D1552057

A SCOOBY-SUMO-SLAM-PACKED ISSUE!
SCOOBY-DOO!™
SUMO A-GO-GO
TERRANCE GRIEP - WRITER
FABIO LAGUNA - ARTIST
HEROIC AGE - COLORS
JOHN J. HILL - LETTERS
VINCENT DEPORTER
COVER
HARVEY RICHARDS
EDITOR
DE PORTER
Spotlight

visit us at www.abdopublishing.com

Reinforced library bound edition published in 2012 by Spotlight, a division of the ABDO Group, 8000 West 78th Street, Edina, Minnesota 55439. Spotlight produces high-quality reinforced library bound editions for schools and libraries. Published by agreement with Warner Bros.—A Time Warner Company. The stories, characters, and incidents mentioned are entirely fictional. All rights reserved. Used under authorization.

Printed in the United States of America, Melrose Park, Illinois.
052011
092011
 This book contains at least 10% recycled materials.

Library of Congress Cataloging-in-Publication Data

Griep, Terrance.
  Scooby-Doo in Sumo a-go-go / writer, Terrance Griep ; artist, Fabio Laguna.
  -- Reinforced library bound ed.
     p. cm. -- (Scooby-Doo graphic novels)
  ISBN 978-1-59961-923-1
  1. Graphic novels. I. Laguna, Fabio, ill. II. Scooby-Doo (Television program)
III. Title. IV. Title: Sumo a-go-go.
  PZ7.7.G75Sbs 2011
  741.5'973--dc22
                                     2011001371

All Spotlight books are reinforced library bindings
and manufactured in the United States of America.

SCOOBY-DOO!

Table of Contents

SUMO A-GO-GO 4

STARS BEHIND BARS 16

SUMO A-GO-GO

THERE YOU ARE! IT FIGURES THAT, DURING TOKYO'S PREMIER SUMO WRESTLING TOURNAMENT, YOU TWO WOULD END UP HERE!

NOM NOM SMK NOM

NOM SMK NOM NOM

TERRANCE GRIEP - WRITER
FABIÓ LAGUNA - ARTIST
HEROIC AGE - COLORS
JOHN J. HILL - LETTERS
VINCENT DEPORTER - COVER
HARVEY RICHARDS - EDITOR

SHAGGY, SCOOBY--YOU KNOW WE'VE GOT TO GET TO THE DOHYO BEFORE THE DOHYO-IRI STARTS!

THE OPENING CEREMONY IN THE WRESTLING RING? LIKE, SORRY, **VELMA**-- WE WERE PURSUING A SOUVENIR FOR SCOOBY AND DECIDED TO TAKE IN SOME JAPANESE CULTURE.

YEAH, THROUGH YOUR MUZZLES!

NOW, VELMA--IS THAT ANY WAY TO SPEAK ABOUT AN ASPECT OF, LIKE, **SUMOTORI** TRAINING?

...CAN...NN... NOT...

...EAT...

...UH... ANOTHER...

...BUHHH...

I GUESS YOU'RE *TECHNICALLY* RIGHT ABOUT THAT. THE EATING OF CHANKO-NABE STEW IS A TRADITION INTENDED TO HELP SUMO WRESTLERS GAIN WEIGHT.

YEAH, IT'S BEEN MY INTENTION TO INQUIRE: WHY DO THEY WANT TO, LIKE, ROUND UP THE POUNDS?

SUMO IS A COMBAT SPORT WHERE THE OBJECT IS FOR THE WRESTLERS TO FORCE EACH OTHER OUT OF THE RING, SO SIZE--NHN! UPSY-DAISY!-- SIZE IS A MAJOR ADVANTAGE.

"AND SPEAKING OF SIZE, OUR *SIZABLE* FRIEND *TOMMY YAMAGUCHI* WANTS TO STEP ONTO THE SUMO PATH."

"...SUMO NEEDS YOU, NEEDS YOUNGER SHOULDERS TO CARRY ITS TRADITIONS..."

OH-OH...LOOKS LIKE THAT PATH IS DEVELOPING A RIKISHI-SIZED BUMP. *KANJIBONO*, THE BIGGEST WRESTLER ON THE ROSTER, IS HAVING WORDS WITH OUR FRIEND...

TOMMY, TRAINING FOR SUMO IS MORE, MUCH MORE DEMANDING THAN YOUR LAST JOB, OVERSEEING THIS VENUE'S MAINTENANCE.

IF YOU WISH TO WALK ALONG THE SUMO PATH, YOU *MUST* BETTER ATTEND. YOU THINK BECOMING BIG MAKES YOU A SUMO.

SIZE IS AN ASSET, BUT *STRATEGY* AND *DEDICATION* ARE MORE IMPORTANT.

I KNOW, KANJIBONO--I AM LOOKING FOR A *HEYA*, A STABLE IN WHICH TO TRAIN...

...BUT ALONE, I CANNOT...

KANJIBONO VERSUS RADEN

TOMMY, ATTEND: TONIGHT I MEET MY ARCHEST OF ARCHRIVALS, THE DIS-HONORABLE RADEN, IN MY FINAL MATCH.

THE EMPEROR'S CUP HAS DISAPPEARED, TOO! BUT THE OTHER PRIZES ARE UNTOUCHED!

...WITH ONE EXCEPTION-- THE GOLDEN SCISSORS IS MISSING, AS WELL. HMMM...

I GUESS... I GUESS THE TOURNAMENT IS CANCELED.

WELL, ISN'T THIS... OPPORTUNE?

RADEN!

IF THE TOURNAMENT IS NEGATED BY THE TENGU, KANJIBONO, YOU'LL BE SPARED THE ABJECT HUMILIATION OF LOSING YOUR LAST MATCH TO ME, HAI?

OR PERHAPS YOU'LL BE SPARED A SIMILAR HUMILITY. HUMILITY IS SOMETHING YOU COULD *USE*, RADEN--

OKAY, YOU TWO...

...IF YOU'RE GONNA FIGHT, I'M GONNA MAKE SURE THAT PEOPLE PAY TO SEE IT.

HA! SPOKEN LIKE THE SHAMELESS PROMOTER YOU ARE, *SUZI TSURUTA!* SUMO WRESTLING ISN'T ABOUT MONEY!

SUMO IS ABOUT HONOR AND TRADITION! PERHAPS YOU'D LIKE TO SEE THE CONTEST CANCELED SO THAT YOU MIGHT PROMOTE MORE AND PROFIT MORE LATER.

WHY, YOU--!

RUIN MY FOUL TATTOO THE BLACK POT OF CHICKEN TO FIGHT FOR GREEDY PRIDE OF--

WELL, GANG--LOOKS LIKE WE'VE GOT A MYSTERY ON OUR HANDS. LET'S LOOK AROUND...

I...I DID AS YOU TOLD ME TO DO, KANJIBONO: I WIELDED STRATEGY AND DEDICATION.

...

HE SURE DID! FOR ONE THING, HE HAD HIS FORMER COLLEAGUES, THE JANITORS, GENERATE THE TENGU'S WIND WITH THIS FAN.

THE TENGU'S FLIGHT WAS ACHIEVED WITH THESE KITE-LIKE FINS.

THIS IS ANOTHER OF HIS FORMER CO-WORKERS, BY THE WAY.

THAT'S-- ≈CHOMP!≈--THAT'S WHY WE, LIKE, BLEW THE CLUES. THE ENTIRE JANITORIAL STAFF CLEANED 'EM UP-- LITERALLY!

THE REAL PURPOSE OF THE CAPER WAS TO STEAL THE GOLDEN SCISSORS, SO AS TO PREVENT KANJIBONO'S RETIREMENT.

STEALING THE EMPEROR'S CUP WAS MEANT TO CONFUSE EVERYONE...

BUT TOMMY-- WHY?

EVEN AS THE SUMOS WERE AFRAID OF THE TENGU, I AM AF...AFRAID TO WALK ALONE ALONG THE SUMOTORI'S PATH. AND I REASONED THAT IF YOU DIDN'T RETIRE, YOU WOULDN'T... I COULDN'T...

...I'M SORRY.

LOCATED ALONG THE NORTHERN NEW ENGLAND COAST, *SENTWORTH PENITENTIARY* IS THE OLDEST *WOMEN'S PRISON* IN THE COUNTRY. BUT PERHAPS NOT FOR MUCH LONGER...

LIGHTS OUT, YOU SLUGS! OFF TO BED WITH YOU AND NO NONSENSE!

HEY, YOU DOWN THERE! NO WANDERING THE HALLS AFTER *CURFEW!*

DIDN'T YOU *HEAR* ME? YOU'RE BREAKING *REGULATIONS!* COME BACK HERE!

IF YOU DON'T RETURN TO YOUR *CELL,* I'LL HAVE TO PUT YOU ON *REPORT!* DON'T CAUSE ANY *TROUBLE* OR--!

‡GASP!‡ OH, MY--!

NO! I WILL *NEVER* RETURN TO MY CELL--EVER AGAIN!

STARS BEHIND BARS

FRANK STROM -writer
SCOTT NEELY -artist
HEROIC AGE -color
JOHN J. HILL -letterer
HARVEY RICHARDS -editor

VERY WELL--AT LEAST *THAT* MAKES SENSE!

JINKIES! SHE SURE IS ONE LADY WHO CAN'T BE *EASY* TO WORK WITH!

TRUE ENOUGH, BUT I'LL PROBABLY END UP *MISSING* HER WHEN THE SENTWORTH IS *CLOSED DOWN.*

CLOSED DOWN? WHAT DO YOU MEAN?

FEDERAL BUDGET CUTS, I'M AFRAID. SENTWORTH PENITENTIARY IS BEING *CLOSED.*

OUR INMATES WILL BE *RELOCATED* TO OTHER PRISONS, AND OUR *GUARDS* WILL BE REASSIGNED. AS FOR *ME*--I'LL BE *UNEMPLOYED!*

ONE OF THE *PRISONERS* HAS TO BE RESPONSIBLE! SOMEONE'S PLANNING AN *ESCAPE* AND USING THE *GHOST* AS A *DISTRACTION!*

BAH! DON'T LISTEN TO *FERGUSON.* IF ANYONE'S PULLING A SCAM, IT'S *HER!* BELIEVE ME!

AND *YOU* ARE...?

BEA BRYANT--"*QUEEN BEA*" TO MY MATES. I'VE BEEN IN THIS DUMP FOR *DECADES* AND KNOW IT ALL!

OL' FERGUSON IS BEHIND PLENTY OF *ILLEGAL ACTIVITIES* HERE, LIKE *GAMBLING.* WHAT BETTER WAY TO COVER HER TRAIL THAN WITH A *GHOST SCARE?*

BEA MAY BE RIGHT, BUT I'VE BEEN READING SOME *HISTORY BOOKS* AND I GET A SPOOKY FEELING WE'RE DEALING WITH *LIZZIE ANDERSON!*

IS SHE, LIKE, ANOTHER *INMATE?*

SHE WAS THE *FIRST* INMATE IN THIS PRISON--CONVICTED OF A CRIME SHE *DIDN'T* COMMIT.

WHERE CAN WE FIND HER?

YOU *CAN'T.* SHE DIED IN 1897!

ALL RIGHT, LET'S GET ON WITH IT. YOU'VE GOT MANY *OTHER* PRISONERS TO SEE--THOUGH I CAN'T IMAGINE *THIS* LOT BEING OF ANY USE.

IT WON'T HURT TO QUESTION THEM ANYWAY-- MAYBE ONE OF THEM SAW SOMETHING.

HOW ABOUT IT, LADIES? DID ANYONE *SEE* ANYTHING LAST NIGHT AFTER CURFEW?

NO, BUT WE'RE GETTING AN EYEFUL *NOW!*

HIYA, CUTIE! WHAT'S *YOUR* NAME?

≈GULP!≈ WHO--*ME?*

DON'T BE *SHY!* WE *LIKE* YOU--A *LOT!*

ER...UH... THAT'S EXACTLY WHAT I'M AFRAID OF--!

HEY, GANG-- DID YOU HAVE ANY LUCK WITH THE INMATES? I WAS TALKING TO SOME ON MY OWN.

NO--ALL WE LEARNED IS THESE ARE *DESPERATE* WOMEN!

I'LL SAY! THEY WERE ALL OVER *SHAGGY* LIKE *LOVESICK TEENAGERS!*

DON'T KID AROUND! THERE'S SUCH A THING AS, LIKE, *TOO MUCH* AFFECTION... ESPECIALLY FROM *HARDENED CRIMINALS!*

THIS ISN'T GOOD--WE'VE GOT NO STRONG *CLUES.* THE ONLY WAY WE'RE GOING TO LEARN ANYTHING ABOUT THE GHOST IS FROM AN *OVERNIGHT STAKEOUT!*

OKAY, I GUESS WE'RE GOING *HUNGRY* TONIGHT!

YOIKS!! RUN FOR IT, SCOOB!

FER-FWANG

SHAGGY, IF YOU WANTED *COMPANY*, YOU COULD HAVE JUST *ASKED*.

COMPANY? WE'VE ALREADY GOT *TOO MUCH* COMPANY--THE *GHOST* IS AFTER US!

DON'T BE SUCH A *BABY!* SHE'S *GONE* NOW!

YEAH, BUT SHE CAN ALWAYS *COME BACK!* IT'S NOT *SAFE!* WE NEED *PROTECTION!* WE NEED TO *HIDE*, AND FAST!

SETTLE DOWN, SHAGGY-- I'VE GOT A *PLAN*.

YOU AND SCOOBY CAN HIDE IN *HERE*--IT'S THE MOST *SECURE* PLACE IN THE WHOLE PRISON.

REALLY? WHAT'S SO *SPECIAL* ABOUT *THIS* CELL?

THE END